Brian Wildsmith

If I Were You

Oxford University Press

Oxford Toronto Melbourne

I went to the zoo,
and I thought. . .

If I were an eagle,

I would fly to the moon.

If I were a walrus,

I would swim to the
bottom of the sea.

If I were a monkey,

I would climb the highest tree.

If I were an elephant,

I would lift a tractor
high into the air.

If I were a cheetah,

I would win every race.

But if you were me. . .

. . .you would be free.

Oxford University Press, Walton Street, Oxford OX2 6DP

Oxford New York
Athens Auckland Bangkok Bombay
Calcutta Cape Town Dar es Salaam Delhi
Florence Hong Kong Istanbul Karachi
Kuala Lumpur Madras Madrid Melbourne
Mexico City Nairobi Paris Singapore
Taipei Tokyo Toronto

and associated companies in
Berlin Ibadan

Oxford is a trade mark of Oxford University Press

© Brian Wildsmith 1987
First published 1987
Reprinted 1988, 1989, 1991, 1992, 1994, 1995

British Library Cataloguing in Publication Data
Wildsmith, Brian
If I were you. — (Cat on the mat)
I. Title   II. Series
823'.914[J]   PZ7

ISBN 0-19-272182-8

Typeset by Pentacor Ltd, High Wycombe, Bucks
Printed in Hong Kong